Consultant: Gussie Hearsey
On behalf of the Pre-school Playgroups Association

First published 1987 in Germany by Loewes Verlag as
Der Bewacher des Honigtopfes

This edition first published 1989 in the United
States by Ideals Publishing Corporation
Nelson Place at Elm Hill Pike
Nashville, TN 37214
Originally published 1988 in Great Britain by
Walker Books Ltd., London

Text © 1987 Norbert Landa
Illustrations © 1987 and 1988 Hanne Türk
English translation © 1988 Patricia Crampton

Printed and bound in Italy by L.E.G.O., Vicenza

ISBN 0-8249-8300-9

BRUIN
The Keeper of the Honeypot

Written by
Norbert Landa

Illustrated by
Hanne Türk

Translated by
Patricia Crampton

Ideals Publishing Corp.
Nashville, Tennessee

"Good morning, Susie Bruin!
Good morning, Bruin!"
called Grandpa Bruin early one morning.
"It's market day again
and we've got lots of cabbages to sell!"

"Oh yes!" cried Susie Bruin,
and she jumped out of bed right away.
"Oooah," mumbled Bruin,
"I feel like a little more sleep today."
"All right," said Grandpa Bruin,
"as long as you won't be bored
with only Fred Parrot for company."

Never, thought Bruin. I'm *never* bored.
Susie Bruin and Grandpa Bruin drove away, and
Bruin waved and yawned. He was still
so-o-o tired. Then he crawled back into bed,
and the next moment he was – wide awake.

However much he tossed and turned
and wriggled and squirmed, his
tiredness had gone for good.
"Good morning, Fred!"
called Bruin. "We'd
better get up!"
But Fred stayed
just where he was.

Bruin felt odd all alone in the kitchen.
"I'm never bored," he said.
"And if I am, I'll play hide-and-seek
with Floppy."
Bruin hid Floppy
behind the bread basket.
He closed his eyes and counted up to eight
and then ran off to look for Floppy.
This is no fun, thought Bruin.

Perhaps it would be more fun
to find out what's in those jars.
This is much more exciting,
thought Bruin as he tasted everything –
crab apple jelly and mustard and pickles
and jam and vinegar
and mayonnaise.
But where is the
honeypot? Bruin
wondered.

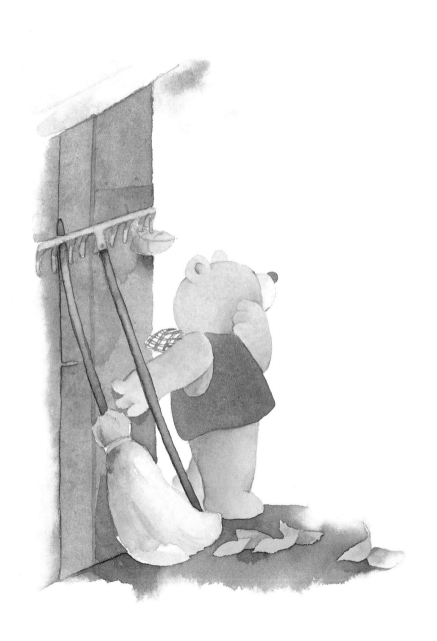

The honeypot was in the shed,
and nobody was looking after it.
Anyone could come and eat it –
a honey robber might even
take it away, thought Bruin.
The honeypot should be in the kitchen!

First Bruin fetched the table from the kitchen.
Then he put a chair on top of the table and
a stool on top of the chair.
The only question was,
how could a small bear
with a big honeypot
ever get down again?

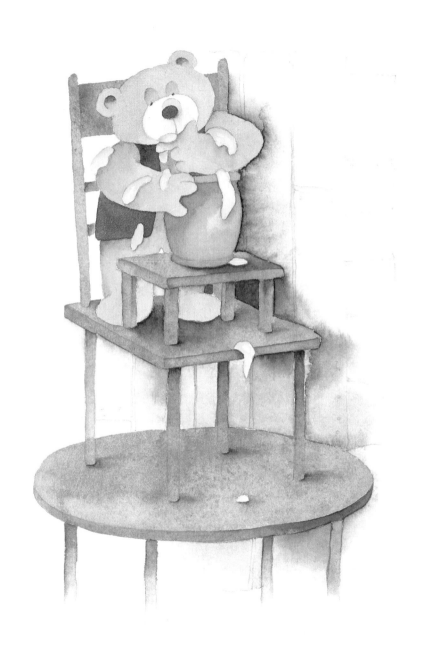

First the stool wobbled;
then the chair wobbled;
then the table began to wobble too.
Bruin thought, if I lick all of the honey
out of the pot, it won't be so heavy
and I can easily jump down!

Soon the pot was empty and Bruin was full
with sticky honey all over him.
"One, two, two-and-a-half, three!" he counted,
then gave himself a shake and jumped
right into the middle of the big,
soft pile of leaves.
"Whew!" said Bruin. "That was lucky!"
When he carried the pot into the kitchen
to keep it safe, Bruin looked like a . . .

". . . monster!" squawked Fred Parrot.
"Monster! Help! Give us a kiss!"
Bruin was at least as startled as Fred.
"But Fred," he stammered, "it's me, Bruin,
the keeper of the honeypot.
Please stop screeching!"

Suddenly there was a loud knock at the door.
Bruin was very frightened.
"Go away!" he shouted. "Who's that in there –
I mean, out there? Robbers! Help!"

"Hey, Bruin," said Grandpa Bruin,
"what *are* you talking about? And
what on earth do you look like?"
"What a funny monster," giggled Susie Bruin.
"Keeping our honey safe, are you?"

"I'm keeping the honeypot safe," said Bruin.
"Not the honey – just the pot!"